PRINCESS KITTY

By Steve Metzger 👑 Illustrated by Ella Okstad

HARPER
An Imprint of HarperCollinsPublishers

200 HarperCollins PUBLISHERS
Since 1817

Princess Kitty
Text copyright © 2017 by Steve Metzger • Illustrations copyright © 2017 by Ella Okstad
All rights reserved. Manufactured in China.
No part of this book may be used or reproduced in any manner whatsoever without written permission
except in the case of brief quotations embodied in critical articles and reviews.
For information address HarperCollins Children's Books, a division of HarperCollins Publishers,
195 Broadway, New York, NY 10007 www.harpercollinschildrens.com

Library of Congress Cataloging-in-Publication Data
Metzger, Steve.
    Princess Kitty / by Steve Metzger ; illustrated by Ella Okstad. — First edition.
        pages cm
    Summary: Believing her life to be much more glamorous than it is in reality, a cat with a big imagination is convinced that a
family surprise party must be for her.
    ISBN 978-0-06-230662-3 (hardcover)
    [1. Cats—Fiction. 2. Princesses—Fiction. 3. Parties—Fiction. 4. Humorous stories.] I. Okstad, Ella K., illustrator. II. Title.
PZ7.M56775Pr 2016   2014048470
[E]—dc23   CIP
                                                                                                                              AC

The artist used pencil and digital coloring to create the illustrations for this book.
Typography by Chelsea C. Donaldson
17 18 19 20 21 SCP 10 9 8 7 6 5 4 3 2 1
❖
First Edition

To Nancy, Julia, and Biscuit —S.M.

To my husband, three children, and our cat —E.O.

My name is Princess Kitty.

My attendants have only one job . . . taking care of ME! They know just what I need.

I live here in this gorgeous palace.

You know, being a royal princess is nothing new to cats.
My ancestors lived in palaces, too.

They even slept on the finest satin pillows—just like me.

Every day the birds sing sweet songs to me.
I love my feathered friends.

And today I found out some exciting news. Two of my attendants are throwing a party in my honor! I'm just crazy about special occasions.

They're trying to keep it a secret, but a smart princess always knows what's happening in her kingdom.

My surprise party is a week away.
I can't wait! Luckily, my daily palace
activities keep me very busy.

On Sunday, my dear friend Princess Puff comes for a royal visit. She arrives in her fancy coach. Ooh la la!

We have so much fun
catching up. I share my
tasty treats

and most beloved toys.

When it's time for
Princess Puff to leave,
I'm just too sad to say
good-bye.

On Monday, I take ballet class and practice my grand jeté. Madam Le Chat always reminds me to keep my tail straight.

On Tuesday, it's the perfect time for a tea party.
Milk or cream?

And going to the theater on Wednesday is such a delight!
I always have the purr-fect seat for the latest show.

On Thursday, I receive a relaxing massage.

It's important to be well rested before a big party.

Oh my! This new attendant seems to need more training.

And on Friday, we eat extraordinary
delicacies from faraway lands. Mmm!

Finally it's Saturday! My loyal attendants are
making sure everything is just right. Shhh. . . .
It's supposed to be a surprise.

Aha! I just heard the doorbell. Attendants, please let my guests in.

Look at all these presents—and they're all for me! What could they be? The latest fashions from Paris? A sparkly necklace?

Oh, it's time for party games! This one is my favorite.

Excuse me, I didn't realize we
were painting now. A princess likes
to be included in all activities.

Well . . . I'll just open one of my presents.

"Oh, Princess Kitty!"

Oops! Ribbons can be tricky sometimes.

"Here's a special necklace just for you."

I knew this would be a grand party.

Just like I told you, the life of a princess is wonderful—and celebrating with friends is the best gift of all.